Allen R. Darrow

Poems of the Gospel

Allen R. Darrow

Poems of the Gospel

ISBN/EAN: 9783337407209

Printed in Europe, USA, Canada, Australia, Japan

Cover: Foto ©Andreas Hilbeck / pixelio.de

More available books at **www.hansebooks.com**

⟩

Poems of the Gospel

Or, Scripture Incidents and Teachings
In Paraphrase and Verse

by
Allen R. Darrow

Illustrated

NEW YORK   CHICAGO   TORONTO
Fleming H. Revell Company
M DCCC XCVII

THE NEW YORK TYPE-SETTING COMPANY

———

THE CAXTON PRESS

CONTENTS

CONTENTS

PREFACE

IN illustrating the various Scripture incidents and teachings in " Poems of the Gospel," the author has found an ample field in the celebrated paintings of ancient and modern artists. Reproductions by photograph in " half-tone " of these works of art, more or less descriptive of the themes considered, are therefore here submitted.

THE AUTHOR.

SONG OF THE EPIPHANY

SONG OF THE EPIPHANY

IN the stillness of an Eastern night,
On Bethlehem hills there shone a light,
  Where shepherds were guarding their sheep ;
A light whose brightness in mystery came,
Inspiring awe in the wondering men
  Who alone the night-watch keep.

A voice fell then on the stillness there,
An angel voice dispelling their fear
  As he hailed salvation's morn.
The glad, glad tidings of the new-born King
In anthems of worship let heaven now ring,
  With praise for a Redeemer born.

A heavenly host come down to earth,
In echoing strains of praise break forth,
  " Peace on earth, good will to man."
With loud hosannas' joyful strain
Celestial voices chant the refrain,
  " Glory to God in the highest."
Through courts of heaven resound the song,
While earth and sky the theme prolong,
  " Peace on earth, good will to man."

CHORUS:
  Now to earth, descent from heaven,
  God the Father Christ hath given.

The Babe is born who, King of kings,
With power divine salvation brings.
   Behold the love of God to man!
   Halleluiah, praise! Amen.

At Bethlehem before Him bow;
Shepherds, come and worship now;
Lo! far and near the tidings tell,
And let the echoes ever swell.
   Behold the love of God to man!
   Halleluiah, praise! Amen.

A SONG OF THE ADVENT

A SONG OF THE ADVENT

O SHEPHERD watch on Judean hills!
What wondrous light is that which fills
Your souls with fear and deep amaze,
As you at midnight heavenward gaze?
O shepherd watch! forget your fear,
And glad the angels' anthem hear.

" Hosanna! we good tidings bring:
At Bethlehem is born your King.
O chosen seed! with glad acclaim
To you we wondrous news proclaim.
Peace on earth—oh, hail the morn!
For lo! a Saviour Prince is born."

Haste, then, O shepherds! bow before
Your King divine and Him adore;
For lo! e'en now, o'er lands afar,
Arisen shines a mystic star,
To point to where the Babe divine
Is born, a King of David's line.

Of David's line, yet, wondrous grace!
A Saviour born for all the race.
Bright star of promise, guide the way
For Gentile wise men, night and day,

As, faith-inspired, they gladly bring
Their costly gifts in offering.

O chosen tribes! O alien bands!
O sons of all far Gentile lands!
He, Prince for all, one sovereign—Lord—
" Good will to men " His gracious word—
Hail, then, your King, O host on host,
And haste millennial Pentecost!

THE WORSHIP OF THE MAGI.

THE WORSHIP OF THE MAGI

Lo! to the Eastern magi, shining afar,
There came the vision of a mystic star,
Pointing to the west its guiding ray,
Toward the humble place where meekly lay
     Jesus, the lowly One.

The wise men journeyed from the Eastern plain,
Inspired with faith by the Spirit's reign ;
In wisdom taught, but not given of earth
To discern the herald of Messiah's birth,
     The hope of Israel come.

To Bethlehem, prophetic, favored spot,
Moved the guiding star, and tarried not
Until it stood o'er the wayside inn
Where in beauty lay the new-born Son,
     Christ, the holy One.

In this humble Child the wise men saw
The promised Shiloh of the Jewish law,
And bowing low, they adoration gave
To Him as King, come with power to save
     The ruined sons of men.

With joyful hearts enlightened from above,
And a faith new-wrought in redeeming love,

They brought their offerings and laid them
    down
At the feet of the Child, and thus did crown
      The prophet's word,

Who in ancient times proclaimed a day
When, given to man in most wonderful way,
There should arise on earth a " Priest and
    King,"
And to a ruined world salvation bring
      As Christ and Lord;

Whose birth miraculous, whose days of youth,
Whose manhood's works and whose words of
    truth,
Whose death and rising by redeeming grace,
To all who believe will assure a place
      In the heaven of God.

IMMANUEL.

IMMANUEL

ALMIGHTY Prince, the Son of God,
   The " Wonderful " in heaven,
Come down to earth to dwell with man;
   Behold a Saviour given.

Jesus His human name is called,
   The sweetest known on earth;
Eternal name, ordained on high
   And given e'er His birth;

A name whose meaning all may know :
   A Saviour for mankind,
High Priest from God, with seal divine;
   His favor all may find.

The aged sinner bowed with guilt
   May to the Lord draw near;
The little child within His arms
   Be folded, free from fear.

All human woes, all human ills,
   Whate'er their natures are,
May all be brought to Jesus' feet;
   He'll then the burden share.

He gives His love; with grace divine
　Doth human prayers attend;
Though sovereign Christ, eternal Lord,
　Man's Saviour, Brother, Friend.

BAPTISM OF JESUS.

BAPTISM OF JESUS

Lo! in the fulfilment of prophetic word,
Through Judean land the stirring voice was heard
Of one who forth from the desert came—
A mighty preacher in Jehovah's name;
A new Elias to waiting people sent
With voice of warning and the cry, " Repent!"
And, faith-inspired, the people all drew near
And listened to his voice with awe and fear.
" Repent! forsake your sins!" rang out his word.
." Repent, and be baptized," the cry was heard;
" Make straight the paths; from evil purge the
    land.
Repent! for lo, His Kingdom is at hand."

    And gathered there on Jordan's shore
      From all the region round,
    The multitudes the witness bore
      To hope and joy they found.

    But One there was, of holy name,
      All undefiled by sin,
    Who also to the prophet came
      To be baptized by him.

    With wondering awe and doubting mind
      The prophet turned away;

" I've need to be baptized of Thee,
 And comest Thou to me?"

" Yet suffer it now," the answer came;
 " All righteousness fulfil.
I here this sacred rite ordain—
 I do My Father's will."

The prophet then, with trembling hand
 And faith inspired anew,
Baptized the Lord at His command,
 God's glory brought to view,

For coming up from out the wave,
 Like a descending dove,
The Holy Spirit witness gave
 With voice from heaven above.

" Behold, My well-beloved Son
 In sovereign grace I give
To die for man—'tis mercy's boon;
 Oh, hear His word, and live."

JESUS TEMPTED.

JESUS TEMPTED

In the lone wilderness, apart from men,
Christ found a conflict with the prince of sin;
When lingering days and nights were passed
In untold conflict and protracted fast,
Neglected nature was aroused at length
To reassert her claim with hunger's strength.
Satan, alert, beholding now his hour,
Sought this advantage for his subtle power,
And to the fainting Lord he wisely said:
" Command the waiting stones that they be
        bread.
Why suffer pangs of a lingering death
When by Thy mighty power, a word, a breath,
The food thou needest shall at once arise
From off the earth in bountiful supplies?
And truly what can be more just and meet
Than that Thy power procure Thee bread to
        eat?"
With firm and searching eye the blessed Lord,
With solemn import in each uttered word,
Rebuked the tempter for his deep offense,
And with this potent truth He drove him
        thence:
" 'Tis written, Man shall not live alone by bread,
But by His sacred word, the truth, be fed."

Not yet o'erthrown by this discouragement,
Nor with this essay of his craft content,
He led the Lord by some mysterious power
Up the temple's height of loftiest tower,
And there, beholding far below their feet
The thronging people of the busy street,
He spake to Jesus by that strong appeal,
The applause of men. Thus by this ordeal
He sought to arouse within His human mind
The strongest motive that is there enshrined.
" The people, aroused by the prophet's voice,
At glad fulfilment waiting to rejoice,
Look for Messias, who with glories near
Shall from on high in mighty power appear.
Now to secure their loyalty and love
Show them this sign : as from the clouds above
To see in majesty their King come down,
As from the highest heaven, to claim His
    crown ;
For is it not written in prophetic word,
His waiting angels shall attend the Lord,
And Thee uphold by sovereign power alone,
Lest Thou Thy foot should dash against a
    stone ? "
But unto Jesus did this guile appear
Light as the day—his hidden purpose clear ;
And with rebuke that he should seek to prove
By word of God His honor, truth, and love,

SATAN REPULSED.

Christ thus to silence, and with deep contempt,
Remanded Satan for his vile attempt:
" Behold, 'tis written in His sacred Word
This law: Thou shalt not tempt the Lord thy
    God."

Yet now once more the wily foe of man,
By this deep essay of determined plan
God's will to thwart, who by redeeming grace
Would give salvation to a fallen race,
Now led the Christ upon high mountain slope
Where nature's ken, with unassisted scope,
Could look afar o'er plain and hill and sea,
And distant lands of Gentile nations see.
There, by some subtle, potent spirit-power
Evoked to aid the vision of the hour,
He brought as with a telescopic view
A panorama of the ages, and threw
Upon it pictures of all coming time,
A map of all nations, of every clime,
With all earth's glories, power, wealth, and
    state,
And vast assemblage of the proud and great.
Now said the devil, with his boasting word
And winsome voice, as he addressed the Lord:
" This boundless realm, this vast domain you
    see,
With all this wealth and power, is given me;

For while the Ruler of the heavenly host
Can of their numbers all allegiance boast,
I have dominion o'er the sons of men;
O'er all the earth in power supreme I reign.
Art Thou a King? and dost Thou hope to gain
Most loyal subjects and a wide domain?
Come to my standard; show allegiance now;
To my authority in act of worship bow;
And all Thou seest I will Thee endower,
By no doubtful conquest or uncertain power,
But by inheritance, eternal, sure,
A royal realm whose glory shall endure."

Such was the promise made, but the hellish
    plea
Met stern rebuke in this unchanged decree:
"'Tis written, God o'er all maintains the
    throne;
Him only shalt thou serve—yea, Him alone."

CHRIST AND NICODEMUS.

CHRIST AND NICODEMUS

A RULER came to Christ by night,
    A man of earnest mold,
One who sought to know the truth
Of teachings that the Lord set forth,
To learn of Him the secret power,
The source of grace unknown before,
    His wisdom's purest gold.

" Rabbi, that Thou art teacher sent from God
    We know, Thy works unfold ;
But is not life's true purpose served
If man is just, with faith preserved ?
If moral law be kept in truth
Through all the life from earliest youth,
    Does he not heaven gain ? "

The blessed Lord read all his heart,
The secret thought, the hidden part ;
With solemn word and searching eye,
This answer gave, the one reply,
    " Ye must be born again."

The ruler with mistaken mind
    And false-conceiving thought
Could not the Saviour's meaning find
    And know the lesson taught.

" Be born again when one is old?
    How thus I cannot see.
To then retrace the path of life
    In nature cannot be.
Be born! how born again? "

" Be born of cleansing, changed within,
Transformed in heart and freed from sin.
This work is wrought by God's own power;
This grace is not of earthly dower;
    Ye must be born again.
Thy love of self and self-conceit
Must all be left at Mercy's feet;
The Holy Spirit on thee pour,
Like water pure, His cleansing power—
    Thus washed, made white and clean.

" Ye hear the sound of rushing wind,
But whence it comes ye cannot find.
Thus doth the Spirit's vital breath
Dwell in the heart transformed by faith;
    Thus is the birth I mean.

" My kingdom none can ever know
    With heart still blind in sin.
'Tis not of earth, nor earth-born power
    Will not earth's glory win.
My scepter as a power within

Subdues the very soul,
Transforms the life, renews the heart,
    Through love's supreme control ;
The love of God,—His love for man,—
    A love by sin unsought,
A love which gives the life for him,
    A sacrifice unbought.
High Priest am I, the altar, too ;
    The Lamb upon it laid,
This all-atoning offering
    Your righteousness is made."

CHRIST'S LESSON OF THE LILIES.

CHRIST'S LESSON OF THE LILIES

CONSIDER the lilies, how they grow;
By their mute voice faith's lesson know.
They toil, nor spin; they simply bloom
And fill the air with soft perfume,
    In nature's beauty glowing.
Yet Solomon, in all his pride,
    The kingly arts bestowing,
Was not arrayed like one of these
    In vales uncultured growing.
If God in nature shows His power
And clothes with beauty bird and flower,
    Their every fortune knowing,
And notes the sparrow's fall from air,
And all His creatures everywhere
    His constant care receiving,
Why then vex life by anxious care,
And smother faith 'neath doubts and fear,
    Scarce e'en His Word believing?
Why troubled thought for daily bread?
He knows your need, and He has said,
    " By faith on Me relying,
In truth ye shall be clothed and fed,
In mercy all your steps be led,
    My love your need supplying."

CHRIST BLESSING LITTLE CHILDREN.

CHRIST BLESSING LITTLE CHILDREN

ONE day, when wearied with the heavy care
That pressed upon His spirit everywhere,—
Had healed the many sick from far around,
And loosed the chains from those by Satan
  bound,—
As evening sun was gilding fair the west,
He sought with His disciples friendly rest.
He to a village came at eventide,
When from their homes, and pressing to His side,
Glad Judean mothers their young children brought,
With touching faith the Master's blessing sought.
But the twelve, with unenlightened zeal,
Would fain deny to them their fond appeal.
Yet Jesus, prizing human love and faith,
Gave them rebuke as this kind word He saith:
" The little ones—forbid them not to come ;
Before my Father's throne for such there's room.
Know this : like them, in humbleness of heart
Ye all must come, to have with Me a part."

Then to His arms, in loving, fond caress,
Each one He took, and each did kindly bless.

Although in outward form no more He stands
To place upon their heads His human hands,

Yet, mothers of all lands and age and name,
Jesus still lives, is now as then the same;
He blesses still, is here and everywhere,
And will regard if now, by faith and prayer,
Your little ones are brought each morn and eve;
He'll weary not, but will your pleas receive.

THE WOMAN OF SAMARIA.

THE WOMAN OF SAMARIA

FROM journeys o'er Judean hill and plain
Jesus set forth, that He might give again
His truth to dwellers in far Galilee,
Through Samaria passing—"as need must be."
   Walking the long and winding way
   With weary, fainting form, one day,
He came to Jacob's well, and sat to wait
Till His disciples brought their needed meat.

A woman from the neighboring city came,
As ancestors for ages did the same—
Came all prepared with pitcher and with rope
To draw from its cool depths the water up.
   Jesus drew near the open brink
   And said to her, "Give Me to drink."
With much surprise, yet not to quite decline,
She said, "Thy nation doth not deal with mine."

The Saviour, not regarding then her plea,
Intent to teach what speedily should be
For highest good, to the wondering woman said:
"Didst thou but know that boon, the gift of God,
   And Who it is that speaks to thee,
   Thou wouldst of Him the asker be;
And with a power thou dost not know
He'd cause His living springs to flow,

Would give thee freely from that well
The water sweet that cannot fail.
Who drinks thy cup shall thirst again,
And find recurring need remain;
Who seeks My fount, and drinks, shall be
From raging thirst forever free."

Again the woman said, more wondering still:
" Art greater than he who gave this well?
The well is ancient, its waters good and pure;
What fountain may exceeding this endure?
    If it be true that Thou canst give
    Such drafts that thirst no more shall live,
A mighty prophet Thou must surely be;
Thy living water now, oh, give to me.

" If prophet of the Lord, then Thou dost know
Where God doth answer prayer and grace bestow.
Thy nation, full of false and proud conceit,
Despise our Gerizim, our temple's seat,
    And tell us with a zeal profound
    God at Jerusalem is found.
But oft in ages past hath gracious Heaven
Our fathers, on our mount, a blessing given."

" Not on thy mount or Zion's hill alone
Does God hear prayer and sacrifices own;
God is a Spirit, and the humble prayer
From heart sincere He answers anywhere.

The contrite heart, both true and meek,
He will accept and even seek;
Thy secret sins do thou at once forsake,
And His forgiving grace by faith partake."

Jesus then showed with His convincing power
His knowledge of her life—its every hour;
Revealed to her the need of cleansing grace,
The fount that flows for all the human race.
   With heart aglow and new-born zeal,
   She thence returned with this appeal:
" Messiah has appeared, our promised Lord;
Go forth with me and hear His wondrous word."

In vain the twelve, now come to Him, did plead
Their purchased food was His most urgent need;
His soul had risen all thought of food above,
Forgetting hunger in His abounding love.
   " Say not the harvest is not near;
   See, it already white appears.
I've meat to eat whereof ye do not know;
'Tis meat My Father's work and will to do."

'Tis harvest still, though Sychar's day is past,
Yea, age on age, and yet doth harvest last;
World-wide the field, though fast 'tis growing
   old.
Haste, reapers, ere the " harvest-home " is told.

The grain doth ripen everywhere,
But ever few the laborers are;
The harvest's Lord, then, must ye pray
To send forth reapers for each day,
That on wide fields no golden grain be passed,
But all be sought, if garnered all at last.

THE PRODIGAL SON.

THE PRODIGAL SON

To show the Father's all-forgiving love,
Christ to the pressing throng this story gave:
" Two sons mature an aged father had.
The younger, with youth's thoughtless impulse,
    said,
' At my control let now that portion be
Which, come of age, the law secures to me.'
'Twas done; nor heeding wisdom's warning voice,
He gathered all, and made this fatal choice:
To leave parental home, its love and care,
And find in stranger land uncertain fare.
Ah yes! the story true is quickly told.
Freed from kind restraint, we him behold,
With reckless daring, hasting deep within
Mad folly's round of pleasure and of sin.
His substance wasted, then from him away
Turned boon companions, friends—ah, false were
    they!
Ere long, reduced to want, in menial state,
Behold him herding swine—a starveling's fate.
Yea, famished now, in rags from head to feet,
He craves as food the husks the swine do eat.

" But lo! a voice is speaking to him now;
He hears, he heeds, yea, thoughtfully doth bow;

And now, in answer to this inward voice,
With hope new-born, he makes this wisest choice:
' I will arise and seek my father's face;
Yea, plead with him, and crave a servant's place;
For as his son in that forsaken home
I may not plead when I shall thither come.'

" Nay, nay ; but see before the open door
That father waiting, watching evermore;
And when beholding at the close of day
The weary pilgrim coming on his way,
Goes forth, the lost, returning one to meet,
And with rich blessing and deep love to greet.
Though sin-defiled, that alien, wandering one,
Repentant now, is welcomed back, a son.

" ' Prepare the feast!' rang out the father's voice.
' The lost is found!   Let all the house rejoice.' "

THE YOUNG RULER WHO CAME TO CHRIST.

THE YOUNG RULER WHO CAME TO CHRIST

A RICH young ruler came to Christ one day,
And this he said: " Good Master, now I pray,
What can I do yet more than I have done,
That eternal life be gained—heaven be won?"

The Lord divine, with true compassion wrought,
And moved by love, the man's conviction sought.
" Why callest thou Me good? One only is the
    Good;
That title none may claim save only God;
To Him belong all honor, highest love,
From dwellers here and all in heaven above.
A ruler thou, and knowest well the law;
The commandments keep, without a fault or flaw."

" Yea, have I kept the law from early youth,
Have justice ever sought, and sought for truth;
Of all that I possess full tithes are set
To clothe and feed the poor. What lack I yet?"

" One thing thou lackest still, and that alone
Bars thee from worship at the heavenly throne:
Thou hast received from God's abounding store
The wealth of earth, and thou dost now implore

That He will add to this the boon of heaven,
As blessing purchased by some offering given.
There is no price that shall divide the heart
'Twixt heaven and mammon, giving each a part;
But in the worship of each loving soul
He brooks no rival, but requires the whole.
All that thou hast go sell and give the poor,
And to heaven's treasure find an open door;
Take this thy cross, leave all, and follow Me;
True riches find—a soul from burden free."

Alas! now to the young man is made known
His heart had to his worldly idol grown;
With unavailing grief he turned away,
Choosing the present above eternal day.

The Christ! the man! at such decision had,
How shall we know which soul was left more sad?

THE WIDOW'S SON

JOURNEYING in Galilee, near to Nain's gate,
Came Jesus, when, lo! in funeral state
A train came forth, and borne upon a bier
There lay a widow's son, to her most dear.
The Saviour's heart, its pity prompt to give,
In secret purpose said, " Her son shall live."
And, as the mournful train drew slowly near,
They heard that Saviour's voice with awe and fear ;
For with authority he came and said,
" Rest here the train—your burden of the dead."
Then, looking on his form with earnest eyes,
He spake : " Young man, I say to you, Arise."
O wonder to the waiting people there !
O His mysterious power shown everywhere !
For now, where'er that parted soul's domain,
To the flesh at once it is restored again.
The form which just before was stark and cold,
With startled senses, now they all behold
Rise up in manly strength to life's full dower,
For lo! life's Lord had said the word of power.

=

AN ACCUSED WOMAN BROUGHT BEFORE JESUS.

AN ACCUSED WOMAN BROUGHT
BEFORE JESUS

To try the Master by Mosaic code,
They brought to Him a woman from her sin;
So would they wrest a sentence on her crime,
Or prove Him one who had contempt of law.
    And this they, tempting, said:
" Master, this woman is a guilty one,
And for her sin the penalty is death;
Saith Moses, 'Such shall be stoned until they die.'
    What sayest Thou?" they said.

Jesus, with a divine regard of law
Of purest type, above sin's outward act,
Law for the soul, each thought and hidden fact,
    Then stooped and wrote upon the sand.
That only writing they alone have read;
    Its meaning as they scanned
Roused shrinking fear, caused drooping eye and
      head
    And flushing cheek of shame;
Nor could they bear the Master's searching look,
That saw each heart and knew sin's lurking nook,
    Though spoken not its name.
This sentence gave He, rising from the ground:
" Let him condemn with whom no sin is found;

Her sin is judged by innocence alone;
Let him whose soul is clean first cast a stone."

Again he stooped to write, when, one by one,
They all went forth and left the two alone.
Then, with divine and matchless purity,
In sweet compassion and with holy love,
He taught the woman penitence and hope,
Led her for needed strength to Source above,
  And bade her sin no more.

LEAVES ONLY.

LEAVES ONLY

WHEN summer sun shone fair in Kedron's vales,
And fleecy clouds hung soft o'er Judean hills,
Jesus went forth from hillside village rest,
Where He had tarried oft, a welcome guest;
    Went toward the city, there to prove
    By many signs His power and love.

With toiling footsteps down the winding way,
With His disciples, near the full-orbed day,
A living fig-tree far aside was seen,
Whose thrifty foliage, fair and full and green,
    Gave sign that fruit should there be met,
    For harvest-gathering was not yet.

Jesus, though Lord of life, had human need
Upon the bounteous gifts of God to feed.
The fig-tree's leaves gave promises profuse
Of ripest fruit abounding for His use;
    But, reaching forth, He thence receives
    No precious fruit—found only leaves.

Henceforth, behold, that living, green-leafed tree
A barren trunk becomes by His decree;
Its outward vesture changed by sovereign power,
The life-source gone, 'tis withered in an hour.

Life in its highest value's found
When fruit as well as leaves abound.

This lesson here by plainest symbol taught,
Whose truth is with most potent value fraught:
'Tis not by leaves, though every branch they fill,
But by our fruit, we serve the Master's will.
   A fair profession oft deceives,
   But truth is found in fruit and sheaves.

So let this question come to each true soul:
Does life bear fruit, or are its leaves the whole?
Joined am I to the Vine; and do I thence receive
A vital force that makes me truly live?
   Then from that Source, if there I cling,
   Will life its rarest fruitage bring;
   But, severed from the Vine, I'll be
   Like a dead branch or withered tree.

THE PHARISEE AND THE PUBLICAN

THE PHARISEE AND THE PUBLICAN

FOR prayer unto the temple came
  A Pharisee one day;
Unto the temple also came
  A publican to pray.

The Pharisee, with tone and look
  Of sanctity and pride,
Said: "Lord, three times a day I fast,
  And oft am purified;

"All tithes to Thee are fully paid;
  Thy law I've sanctified—
Not like that sinner standing there,
  So wretched and defiled,
Whose every act has been of sin
  Since he was but a child."

The publican, with humble mien
  And attitude of shame,
Cried unto God in penitence,
  As he invoked His name.

"O God, be merciful," he cried,
  "And wash away my sins!"
I tell you, now, before His throne
  This man was justified,

While he whose proud self-righteousness
   No sin of heart could hide
Was unabsolved; for, be it known,
   God ever hateth pride.

He loves the sinner who his sins
   Hath honestly confessed,
And lifts the prayer of penitence,
   In humble faith expressed;
And from the trembling, contrite one
   His grace shall ne'er depart;
Above all outward sanctity
   Is lowliness of heart.

Not, like the world, by outward state
   Does God a judgment give.
The rich are poor, the poor are rich;
   Though dead, the righteous live,
While he who dies is more than dead
   If he depart in sin.
A perfect judgment undeceived
   Discerns the state within.

TEACHING THE MULTITUDES

TEACHING THE MULTITUDES

SEEING on the hillside and the open plain
The shepherds leading to their folds again
Their flocks, to guard from impending harm
Of prowling foe or dangerous alarm,
By clear similitude again He sought
Deep to implant the potent truths He taught.
" I am the Shepherd; hear ye all My voice,
My leading follow, make Me now your choice.
I am the door; by Me now enter in;
Within My fold be safe from death and sin."

The people, filled with wonder strange, profound,
Now gathered near, and crowding, pressing round,
With sudden impulse they this query gave:
" Are they but few Thy blessed truth shall save?"
The Lord divine, discerning all implied,
With sad but yearning love, in answer cried:
" From subtle snares of Satan and of sin
Strive hard, each one, oh, strive to enter in!
When shuts the door, and mercy's day is past,
Many will seek, and be denied at last.
Eternal life, salvation full and free,
Excluding none, I offer now to thee.
Oh, take the gift! Oh, now accept, to-day!
Why still reject My word? Oh, why delay?

Alas! alas! while yet there's time and room,
So hard your hearts, ye will not, will not come.
But oh, beware, My warning voice now heed;
The Spirit will not always strive and plead.
Him grieved away, ye choose a certain doom;
Except He calls, ye cannot, cannot come."

To Pharisees and all remaining near
Again He spake—nor was restrained by fear:
" Why seek the mote within thy brother's eye,
Thy neighbor's fault with sternest voice decry?
Behold a beam thine evil eye within,
Blinding the sight to thine own darker sin.
Man's judgment's bound to outer sense and sight,
Nor can discern the Spirit's inner light.
'Tis by the fruit that every tree doth bear
That its true life and value doth appear;
For, as the thorn can never grapes produce,
Nor bearing figs the thistle prove of use,
As from a fountain bitter thou mayest know
There never can the sweet, pure waters flow,
So from a soul corrupt and foul within
Must ever flow the turbid streams of sin.
Make, then, the fountain pure, and good the tree;
Sweet then the streams, and good the fruit shall be.
When on a house that's built upon the sand
The blasting winds and raging storms descend,
T'will surely fall, nor will destruction stay

'Till by the flood 'tis wholly washed away ;
But if the house is built upon a rock,
'Twill then endure the tempest, flood, and shock.
Then let the house of hope and faith's sure ground
Upon the solid rock of truth be found."

=

CHRIST'S TEACHING OF PRAYER

CHRIST'S TEACHING OF PRAYER

BE not as they who utter sounding words,
For such reward as praise of men affords,
Upon the street or in the market-place,
In forms of prayer, with sanctity of face.
Not thus is prayer, not this to God the way.
Though voice be silent, in spirit ye may pray,
In secret with the Father your weakness own,
Apart from men, to Him your wants make
    known,
And He who scans the closet of each heart
In love and power will then His grace impart;
He at faith's cry will help divine afford,
And with true riches openly reward.
  As children coming, when ye pray
    Our heavenly Father, say:
 "Father all glorious, Thy throne in heaven,
    Source of all blessing given,
 Hallowed be Thy name. Thy kingdom come.
    Thy will on earth be done,
 Thy worship be on earth in love,
    As now in heaven above.
Give us, O God, our daily bread;
    By Thee our souls be fed.
As we forgive, do Thou our debts forgive.
    May grace within us live,

Lest temptings come too strong to bear;
    Save us from Satan's snare.
In weakness be our strength within;
    Keep us from every sin.
The power is Thine, and glory now,
    And we in homage bow.
Save us in heaven at last; we then
    Shall nobler worship give.   Amen."

THE LESSON OF CHARITY

GIVE not thine alms with trumpet blare,
  Nor yet with outward show;
For God regards the loving heart
  And doth its secret know.

Judge not with hard and cruel mind
  Thy neighbor's faults or sin;
For every cause there's One to judge;
  'Tis He who looks within.

Not once, or thrice, or seven times
  Thy brother's fault forgive,
But let a meek, forgiving love
  In thee forever live.

And higher yet, this crowning grace,
  This brightest virtue, know:
Thy bitter foe, whate'er his fault,
  On him thy love bestow.

WALKING ON THE SEA

WALKING ON THE SEA

THE Holy One of God, yet man, He was, of
    prayer;
Oft in solitude He sought the Father's care.
On mountain height alone, no midnight chill
Or damp of dewfall could His fervor still.
There with His God, with conscious need He
    sought
That power divine by which alone He wrought.
As thus for strength He came to God to plead,
And grace for man with Him to intercede,
The Father heard—yea, He accepted there
The precious incense of that midnight prayer.

Then in the early dawning of the morn,
Whose tender rays might well His form adorn,
With face still radiant from the mount of prayer,
Jesus went down again to toil and care;
Went forth, and, walking on the sea, drew near
To His disciples, who, in doubt and fear,
Made toilsome effort and with laboring hand
Sought through the night on farther shore to land.

With straining vision in the morn's dim light
They saw as man a spirit of the night
Walking upon the sea, and drawing near;
The mystic specter filled their souls with fear.

Then Christ, in accents of the tenderest love,
Gave hail, with lifted voice the winds above,
Calming their fear as quickly this He said:
" 'Tis I, your Master, come; be not afraid."
Then of their number that impetuous one
Called, " Bid me come to Thee. Why Thou
    alone?"
Jesus, to teach a lesson that should be
For future profit, said, " Come forth to Me."
Peter went forth and walked upon the sea;
Boldly he went, until the sea's rough wave
Caused faith to wane. He then, in terror, gave
The anxious cry, " I perish, Lord! Oh, save!"
Christ held forth His hand—lo! firm again the
    wave.

The lesson here to every thoughtful mind
Is made most plain: for man shall ever find
That while on Jesus rests the eye of faith,
The child of God in life safe conduct hath;
But when faith's eye from Him is turned away,
Life's raging sea will then to fear betray.
Unless His help comes forth, His arms to save,
The soul, in terror, sinks beneath the wave.

THE RICH MAN AND LAZARUS

THE RICH MAN AND LAZARUS

A RICH man once, in royal state,
  Fared sumptuously each day,
With purple robe and vesture fine,
  And manner proud alway.

Of Abram's seed by record true
  His lineage was traced;
Nor was it said of him that he
  The outward law transgressed.

But there, alas! all title ceased;
  By faith he was not known;
God's grace upon his heart was not,
  Nor blood that could atone.

A poor man, too, there was, well known,
  Whom fortune favored not;
With sores his form was covered o'er,
  And helpless was his lot.

The rich man's gate he haunted oft,
  His fallen crumbs to eat,
While only dogs for ministrants
  The hapless one could greet.

And he was, too, of Abram's seed
  By natural descent;

But in his heart God's grace had sealed
  The Spirit's covenant.

The rich man died—with pride and show
  By thronging friends entombed;
And in the world of woe at once
  His soul its place assumed.

The poor man died—earth's sorrows o'er,
  No earthly pageant given;
But him behold, with Abram blessed,
  Rejoicing, rich in heaven.

THE TRANSFIGURATION

THE TRANSFIGURATION

APART from Syria's mountain-range is seen
One lofty peak that rises from the plain.
With the chosen three, Peter, James, and John,
Jesus ascended once its crest upon;
And there, before their gaze, by wondrous might
His form was changed: His face, in radiance
      bright,
Shone as the sun, or a more glorious light,
And all His garments gleamed in dazzling white.
And when the three, these favored sons of men,
With trembling awe, yet clearest vision, then
This glory saw, new wonder added: now, behold,
Two forms, descending from the heavenly fold,
Talking with Jesus, there before them stood,—
Two ancient prophets, servants of the Lord,—
While from the bright o'ershadowing cloud
The Sonship was declared once more aloud.

Why came this vision?   What the lesson taught?
How is this wondrous scene with mercy fraught?
Why from the spirit-world are seen again
These prophets on the earth?   And why should
      men
Behold the scene?   What doth the vision mean,
With Christ transfigured standing there between?

This glimpse of glory seen through " gates ajar,"
This voice from heaven, and this light afar
Add now another link to faith's strong chain,
To bind in full assurance trustful men—
A demonstration that the just who die
Do yet most surely live with God on high.
It shows in type and prophecy to men
That, though the body perish, yet again,
Joined to the soul, in glory it shall live,
And praise eternal to the Saviour give.

APOSTROPHE TO PETER

THOU bold apostle, how didst thou fulfil
Thy promise, made in strength of native will?
Where was thine armor? where thy sword and
    spear?
Before a feeble foe why didst thou quake and fear?
Alas! thy human firmness and thy boasted
    strength,
While unsustained of grace, gave way at length.
Peter thy name,—the adamantine rock,—
Yet couldst not withstand temptation's shock,
But in the hour of His imputed shame
Thou didst in fear deny thy Master's name.
But when with one sad look of tenderest love
That gentle Master did thy fault reprove,
Thy love, no longer overborne by fears,
Yielded in anguish, penitential tears.
How like the blessed Master to forgive,
And say in pitying mercy, " Rise and live.
With new-born faith, declare My name abroad;
Go forth and feed My sheep, the flock of God."
O native strength! O boast of human power!
When left alone, how false and weak the dower!
" Sifted as wheat," thy sin wrought not despair;
Faith triumphed still—for lo! thy Saviour's prayer.

APOSTROPHE TO JUDAS

APOSTROPHE TO JUDAS

AND thou, O Judas, what can language say
To one who could his blessed Lord betray?
" One of the twelve," with high committed trust,
What evil spirit filled thy soul with lust,
Which, unsubdued by faith and watchful prayer,
Was left to grow and gain possession there,
Until, forgetting all thy Master's love,
Thou couldst for meager gain a traitor prove?
The Prince of Evil, failing to subdue
The Lord of Life, had easy power o'er you.
But, as at first sin came by evil choice,
When Adam disobeyed the Father's voice,
Thy course did show this truth remaining still:
No sin is wrought but by consent of will.
Thou canst not, then, retire behind the plea
That thou wert made to sin by God's decree.
Nay; when the deed was done, the treachery
    paid,
There yet remains this truth.   Deep stains may
    fade
If but remorse be changed to faith and prayer,
And penitence arise from dark despair.
Such was redemption that from thy dark sin
That blood sold for a price could wash thee
    clean.

Alas! the human will, how weak in power
When bound by Satan in temptation's hour!
Though sin overwhelmed thy soul in guilty
    force,
Its fruit, not penitence, but wild remorse.

GETHSEMANE

GETHSEMANE

'TWAS night; silence reigned in Gethsemane;
Nature's time of peace and rest had fallen. Then,
In heaviness of heart and anguished soul,
The Saviour sought the place, apart from men.

Oft had He thither come, with loving friends,
For rest from weariness and strife and care;
For faithful teaching of His truth divine;
For holy converse; more than all, for prayer.

But now, though loving friends were near,
In heaviness of heart, apart, alone,
His complex nature, human and divine,
His agony confessed, with tear and groan.

Sin's awful condemnation on Him fell,
Whose bitter cup, with fullness running o'er
To its last drop, 'midst fainting, faltering prayer,
He now must wholly drink, and ne'er forbear.

In vain, with highest impulse of the mind,
We seek to sound the overwhelming flood
Of that soul's passion, and the breaking heart,
Wringing from His bent form great drops of blood.

Nor can we wonder that in human flesh
E'en Christ should seem to fail with fear, appalled

At that ordeal, a Father's hiding face,
As though on Him the wrath that justice called.

While thus His soul bowed 'neath its heavy load,
Its yearning hope sought balm in human love,
Craved sympathy's support and friendship's aid;
Like broken reeds, they no support could give.

But when, through loving angel ministrants,
New strength was given and full victory won,
The cry arose, key-note in every prayer,
" Thy blessed will alone, O God, be done."

Then heavenly calmness settled on His brow,
As forth He went, through all the ordeal night
In strength and peace, by unseen power sustained,
And soul uplifted to His throne of light.

A VISION OF THE CRUCIFIXION

A VISION OF THE CRUCIFIXION

THOUGHT hath no limit, is not bound by time.
Centuries ago I stood 'neath balmy trees
That grew upon a high and rocky hillside;
Before me spread in its terraced beauty
An ancient city—opulent of wealth,
Favored of God, proud in temple glory.
Thronging the streets were teeming multitudes,
As if there gathered for some sacred feast.
When the sun had risen near noontide height,
Suddenly from out the city gate poured forth
A motley and tumultuous host—soldiers,
Priests, citizens, both men and women,
Strangers from neighboring and distant lands.
Some were clamorous of deep hate and passion;
Others loud wailing, as with sorrow burdened;
While in the midst I beheld One condemned,
Wearing upon blood-stained brow a crown of
    thorns.
I saw Him weary beneath the burden,
Bearing His cross toward the chosen place
Where robbers, murderers, had execution.
And when nearer I looked upon His face,
I was filled with wonder and strange awe of
    soul;
I saw Him, though suffering, calm and patient,

Whose sorrowing face, though marred by care,
Was lit with glory and a heavenly peace.

I followed the passing throng of people
To where, with two thieves, one on either side,
They prepared His place of execution.
I saw Him with arms extended on the cross,
As then, through hands and feet, with brutal force,
The unresisting victim was nailed fast,
While from His lips I heard this breath of
    prayer:
" Father, forgive them, for they know not what
    they do."
Then was He lifted to the gaze of all,
While, half suppressed, yet forced from tortured
    frame,
I heard, amid the tumult, groans of anguish,
As through long hours of mortal suffering
He there endured the ignominy and pain,
The untold agony, of crucifixion.
I heard the jest and sneers of enemies,
As mockingly they cried, " Hail, King of the
    Jews!"
" If God will save Him, let Him now come down,
And by that token we will then believe."
And then, with impulse born of unbelief,
They gave unwitting testimony of truth:
" Others He saved; Himself He cannot save."

IN THE HOUR OF DEATH

Then heard I the passing multitudes—
The voice of some who but the week before
Had hailed Him as the chosen One of God,
And with hosannas loud proclaimed Him king.
Now, with fickle heart and leering gibe, cast
Reproach upon Him as a guilty one.
Now they esteemed Him stricken, afflicted,
Smitten of God, and turned their faces from Him,
Forgetting His wondrous acts of sovereign power,
His holy words and loving ministrations.

Beyond the throng of citizens and soldiers
Were groups of sorrowing friends and followers
And wailing women, who sought against rude
      force,
With loving impulse, nearness to the cross;
And one was she whom, in His wondrous grace,
God ordained elect to be His mother.
Forgetting self, with thoughtful, pitying love,
He spake to her words of cheer and comfort.
Slowly passed the hours of this dark tragedy,
And gathering drops of dampness gave the sign
Of approaching dissolution.   Suddenly,
Moved by agony of soul, deeper, darker
Than all conception of the human mind,
There arose aloud the cry from breaking heart,
" My God, My God, why hast Thou forsaken Me?"
Oh, that awful cry, fathomless in import!

The immaculate, the innocent of God,
By His free mediatorial offering,
The victim of law, its justice and judgment,
Striving through o'ershadowing, veiling cloud
To behold the Father's all-approving smile.
O dreadful woe, the awful curse of sin,
That made for Him the dark cloud possible!

Thus passed the hours, and came the closing scene,
When, lo! again, as by the inspiration
Of last triumphant and exultant thought,
Loud and clear from the expiring victim
Came the cry, "It is finished," and behold,
The scene was closed. He bowed His head in
    death.

Then, lo! the temple's veil was rent in twain—
No more need of sacrificial offerings,
Of blood of beasts, of burning fat, for sin;
Upon the mediatorial cross there hung
The atoning Lamb, God's only Lamb, now slain.

"It is finished"—these last compendious words
Seemed to echo through all the cycles
Of past ages back to the birth of man;
Borne on the wings of time, they seemed to sound
Through ages future, till time on earth shall end;
To reach the ears of the long-forgotten dead,

The millions of the fabled underworld;
They seemed to rise in swelling notes triumphant
Until they sought the very throne of God.

While thus I thought upon these potent words,
Strange and mysterious darkness gathered there,
Spreading a cloud of gloom upon the scene:
The earth shook as by some mighty impulse;
The rocks were rent; and the sepulchers of many,
Long since there buried, gave forth their occu-
    pants.
Men were moved to sudden awe and fear:
Some smote their breasts in dread remorse;
Others cried, " Surely this was the Son of God,"
And with blanching cheek ran and hid away.

" Finished " ! The awful price of man's redemp-
    tion,
Lo, in the blood of Christ is fully paid.

IT WAS FOR ME

FOR sin of man the Christ was slain,
The " Lamb of God," free from all stain.
" For sin of man "—ah yes, for me
It was He died upon the tree;
For me that mournful, broken sigh,
For me that last expiring cry,
      " Eloi, Eloi,
        Lama sabachthani ? "

O midnight anguish unto death!
O Calvary's last expiring breath!
O law of God! it was my sin
That veiled as cloud God's face within,
And from Christ's heart wrung mournful sigh,
His fathomless and awful cry,
      " Eloi, Eloi,
        Lama sabachthani ? "

O thou my soul, by Christ's blood bought,
Do thou thy all, by God's grace taught,
Thy faith, thy love, henceforth Him give,
Thy all of life henceforth Him live.
Through rended veil to God brought nigh,
Forget not e'er that cross-borne cry,
      " Eloi, Eloi,
        Lama sabachthani ? "

EASTER SONG

EASTER SONG

LET the angels of heaven sing pæans of praise;
Let glorified spirits the glad anthem raise;
Let the militant church on the earth join the song,
Uniting in worship, hosannas prolong:
    For He is alive who was slain—
    Lo! Jesus hath risen again.

Let the cornet and harp of melodious sound,
With the loud-pealing organ, send echoes around,
While the worshiping people the tidings pro-
    claim—
Redemption, salvation, in His blessed name:
    For He is alive who was slain—
    Lo! Jesus hath risen again.

Let the church in all ages rejoice for the night
Of Calvary's gloom, that was followed by light,
And the Saviour's glad triumph o'er death and
    . the grave,
Victorious seal of His full power to save:
    For He is alive who was slain—
    Lo! Jesus hath risen again.

Let the high and the low, let the rich and the poor,
Accept full salvation by this open door;

Since Christ the Redeemer, exalted on high,
Bestows this free grace on all who apply :
     For He is alive who was slain—
     Lo! Jesus hath risen again.

Let the birds of the air, let the waves of the sea,
Let the rills of the mountain, the winds o'er the lea,
Let the sun and the cloud, let the stars of the night,
With the whole of glad nature, in carols unite :
     For He is alive who was slain—
     Lo! Jesus hath risen again.